KT-372-095

Gráinseach an Déin
Deansgrange Library
Tel: 2850860

BAINTE DEN STOC

WITHDRAWN FROM
DÚN LAOGHAIRE-RATHDOWN COUNTY
LIBRARY STOCK

Breakfast

Story by Monica Hughes
Pictures by Jim Kavanagh

OXFORD
UNIVERSITY PRESS

I went to see the cows.

2

Cows

I said, "**Breakfast!**"

3

I went to see the sheep.

"**Breakfast!**" I said.

I went to see the goats.

"**Breakfast!**" I said.

I went to see the horse.

Horse

"Breakfast for you!"
I said.

I went to see the hens.

I said,
"Breakfast for you!"

I like eggs.

"Breakfast for me!" I said.